SCOOP
the Digger!

Big thanks to Clare and Pauliina
D.W.

Fizz the shy fire engine

Scoop the boastful digger

Chug the helpful tractor

Choo the forgetful train

ISBN 0-439-74269-2

Text and illustrations copyright © 2003 by David Wojtowycz. All rights reserved.
Published by Scholastic Inc., 557 Broadway, New York, NY 10012, by arrangement with Orchard Books.
SCHOLASTIC and associated logos are trademarks and/or registered trademarks of Scholastic Inc.

12 11 10 9 8 7 6 5 4   6 7 8 9 10/0

Printed in the U.S.A.   40

First Scholastic printing, February 2005

SCOOP
the Digger!

David Wojtowycz

Scholastic Inc.

New York Toronto London Auckland Sydney
Mexico City New Delhi Hong Kong Buenos Aires

Scoop the digger thought that he did
the best job on the building site.

He loved to dig the deepest holes.

DIG! DIG!

He loved to show off
his super-strong arm.
"Look what I can do!"
he boasted.

Tipper the truck went by, carrying a heavy load of sand.

"What an easy job you have!" said Scoop.

"You try it!" replied Tipper, pouring out his sand.

RUMBLE! RUMBLE!

"Okey-dokey," said Scoop.
But he could only pick up
a little bit of sand at a time.

He tried to push the cement,
but it was too runny.

Uh-oh!

whoosh!

Scoop was clear of the cement!

"Thank you!" said Scoop. "And I'm sorry I was bossy. Your jobs aren't easy at all."

"Neither is digging," said Tipper.

"But Scoop, today you were so busy doing our jobs you forgot your own!" smiled Tumble.

They all laughed.